Lew & Quackers

Story by Luisa Battimelli
Illustrations by Renzo Roblodowski
Color & Layout by Nick Infante

First Edition, copyright (c) 2007, Luisa Battimelli,

ISBN: 0-9786232-0-7

Library of Congress Control Number: 2007902606
Publisher: BookSurge, LLC
North Charleston, South Carolina

One sunny afternoon at Elmwood Elementary school, Ms. Snow's class had show and tell. All the boys and girls brought in their favorite things. Mickey brought his pet hamster, Abbey brought in her favorite bed time story, and Lew brought in her favorite stuffed ducky, "Quackers". Lew loved Quackers since the day her daddy bought him for her. When it was Lew's turn to get up in front of the classroom, she stood up with Quackers.

"This is Quackers", said Lew. "He's my best friend in the whole wide world. He is just the right size. Big enough to cuddle, but small enough to go everywhere with me. I love him so much."

After class that day, Lew and her friend Abbey went to the playground. They both decided to go play on the monkey bars for a while. Before Lew went on the monkey bars, she walked over to the bench, and set Quackers down. "Okay Quackers, I'll be right back", said Lew. "I want to play on the monkey bars for a few minutes."

When Lew was done playing on the monkey bars she walked back over to the bench. "QUACKERS, WHERE ARE YOU?!" Lew started to scream out while she was looking all over the bench and the floor for her duck. "Someone took my Quackers!"

Abbey heard Lew crying for Quackers and ran over to her.
"What happened Lew?"
"Quackers is missing!" Lew replied crying.
"I'll help you find him." Abbey said trying to make her friend feel better.

4

Both Lew and Abbey started to look for Quackers. "Where could my ducky be? All I did was place him down on the bench for a few minutes."

"I don't know. Let's start asking around." Abbey told Lew.

They started to ask all the children in the playground if they had seen Quackers.

"Have you seen Quackers?" Lew asked Bobby, who was playing in the sandbox.

"Nope," answered Bobby. "You should ask Jimmy. He knows everything that happens in the playground."

"Jimmy? But he's the playground bully!" Abbey said.

"I know he is, but he always knows everything."

"Fine. We'll ask," said Lew.

Lew and Abbey started to look around for Jimmy, and once they spotted him they walked over to him.
"Hey Jimmy. We've got to ask you some questions," said the girls as they walked towards him.

"Yeah, what do you want?"
"Lew's toy duck Quackers, is missing. Have you seen him?"
"Maybe I did and maybe I didn't," answered Jimmy.

"Well, tell us what you know," said Lew, hoping she would get an answer from him.

"Why should I?"

"Because I love my Quackers. I miss him."

"I'll tell you what you want to know if you do me a favor."

"What's the favor?"

"I lost my favorite baseball. If you find my baseball, I'll tell you where your silly duck is."

"Ok, deal."

Abbey and Lew went to look for Jimmy's baseball. They saw Jenny and Nelly playing hop-scotch and asked them. "Do you girls know where Jimmy's baseball is?"

"No we haven't seen it," said Jenny, "but ask Mickey. He's playing basketball."

"Yeah, Mickey might know," said Nelly.

Abbey and Lew went looking for Mickey and when they found him on the basketball court they asked him, "Have you seen Jimmy's baseball?"
"Yeah."
"Ok, good. Can you tell us where it is?"

"Sure. I saw it about an hour ago. Jimmy's dog Spike was chewing on it."

"Chewing?" Abbey repeated with fear.

"Yeah, chewing", said Mickey. "He was under the big oak tree ripping it apart. That dog rips everything apart once it gets its dirty paws on it."

"Thanks so much Mickey!" Lew said.

Abbey and Lew went to the big oak tree and found Jimmy's baseball ripped apart.

"What are we going to tell Jimmy?" Abbey asked Lew.

"What can we tell him? We have to tell him the truth."

The girls walked back to where Jimmy was playing.
"Hey Jimmy we found your baseball. Now tell me where Quackers is."
"You found my baseball? Give it to me!"
"Here," Lew said as she tossed the baseball to Jimmy.
"What happened to my favorite baseball?"

"Your dog Spike got to it, that's what happened."
"My dog, huh? Well, he also got to your silly Quackers."
"He what?" Lew exclaimed, as she started to cry.

"Spike ran over and grabbed your duck after you put him down on the bench. And, well, you know the rest from there." Jimmy said as he started to grin.

"I'm sorry Lew," Abbey said as she hugged her.

"So am I!" Lew sobbed.

Lew and Abbey started to walk back home.

"What are you going to tell your daddy?" Abbey asked with curiosity.

"I don't know, but he'll be really upset."

"Maybe he'll buy you a new stuffed Quackers," Abbey said with a positive attitude.

While the girls were talking, they passed by a pond.
"Hey Abbey, I bet that pond has ducks," Lew said as she walked towards the pond.
"Hey, where are you going?!" Abbey yelled out as she started to run after her friend.
Once Lew reached the pond she saw a family of ducks.
"Aren't they pretty duckies?", Lew was telling Abbey as she jumped into the pond to catch a baby ducky.

"What are you doing?" Abbey yelled out. "You're going to get hurt!"

"No, I won't. I'm just going to get me another Quackers."

Lew started to chase after the ducks. They were running from left to right, back and forth. The ducks were making so much noise. All you heard was "Quack, Quack, Quack!" Lew tripped, and fell into the water. As she fell in she caught a baby duck. "Now, I got you!" Lew said as she rushed out of the pond with the baby duck in her hands.

"Lew! Watch out! Behind you!" Abbey yelled out.
Lew looked behind her and saw a mad mommy duck chasing after her.
"The mommy duck is mad!!", Abbey screamed.
Lew ran as fast as she could, while the mother duck chased after her. "What am I going to do?" Lew yelled to Abbey. She was very scared.

"Drop the baby duck!" Abbey yelled back.
"No, I want him."

Lew ran past the pond and into the little park area. "I have to hide, I have to hide." Lew said looking for a hiding spot. "I got it!"

Lew saw a garbage can and crawled in it. The baby duck started to cry for its mother. "No, stop crying." Lew said as she covered the duck's bill.

Minutes later, Lew peaked out of the garbage can and didn't see the mommy duck. "Good. She's gone."
Lew crawled out, and saw Abbey sitting on a bench waiting for her.
"Hey Abbey, I lost its mommy."

"I know you did, but that wasn't right. The poor ducky must miss its mommy."
"I'm its new mommy. He'll be fine."

The girls went home. When Lew walked into her house, she went over to her father.

"Daddy, Daddy. Look at what I got!"

"Lew, what happened to you? You're a mess!"

"I got a real ducky."

"What happened to Quackers, and where did you get this duck?"

"Spike, the dog, got to my Quackers, and I got this ducky at the pond."

"Lew, that ducky doesn't belong here with us. It belongs with its own family in the pond."

"Yes, he belongs here with us."

"No Lew, he doesn't. You're a big girl now. You need to learn to let go of things and taking another duck from it's family is wrong.

Quackers is gone, and now you have to prove you're a big girl and go on without him. This ducky needs its mommy. The mommy is heart-broken. I'd be heart-broken if someone took you away from me."

"No, I want to keep him."

"Lew, how did you feel when you found out Quackers was missing?"
"I was sad and mad."

"That's how that ducky's mommy feels right now." Lew's daddy bent down and looked her right into the eye. "The right thing to do is bring him back. Just look at the ducky. He's sad."
Lew saw the ducky's sad eyes, and then told her daddy. "I guess you're right."

They both took a walk over to the pond, and found the ducky's family.
"Now Lew, put him in the pond."

Lew put the ducky in the pond. As soon as Lew let go of him, he flew over to his mother.
"That was a brave thing to do little one", Lew's daddy said. He gave her a big hug.

The next day at school, Lew was playing with Abbey at the playground during recess.

"So, your daddy made you bring the ducky back?" asked Abbey.

"Yeah, ducky was sad."

While the girls were playing and talking, Jimmy walked over to them.

"What do you want Jimmy?" Lew asked angrily. "There aren't more ducks here for you to feed your dog."

"I'm sorry that Spike ate your duck."

"You are?" Lew said in shock.

"Yes, I am. Here, I went to the toy store last night, and bought you a new Quackers." Jimmy handed Lew over the stuffed duck.

"Wow that's nice of you," Lew said as she was hugging her new Quackers. "So, you aren't that much of a bully then?"

"Shush...don't tell anyone," Jimmy said as he winked at Lew. "I like being in charge. I'm no softy."

The End

www.ingramcontent.com/pod-product-compliance
Lightning Source LLC
Chambersburg PA
CBHW041544240626
47164CB00002B/122